My Real Family

To my dear husband Ken, who has invested his life in learning and teaching
—from Graci.

My dad is going to get married to a lady who has two girls. Yuk!

When we go over to her house on Saturday, my dad watches cartoons with the girls. He's too busy to do that with me. I don't know why he wants to get married again. We're getting along just fine by ourselves. Aren't *I* enough?

Why did my parents have to get divorced? They fought a lot, but who doesn't?

Mom is mad because Dad keeps talking about how happy he is now. I ride the bus to my mom's house every weekend. Her house is small and I don't have a bedroom of my own, so I sleep on the couch. I do have a dresser all to myself, though.

As soon as I get there, she asks me about Dad. I hate that because I never know what to tell her. I wish she would ask me about ME.

Now that my dad is getting a new family, he might not want me to live with him. Mom says she can only take care of me on weekends. What if I don't have a place to live?

Last weekend Mom gave me a letter to give to my dad. It made him mad. She asked him for more money, but he said he didn't have more money now that he is getting another family.

Sometimes I worry that I caused the divorce to happen. But mostly I worry about my dad getting married again and me living with two girls!

I told my dad that I wanted him to marry my mom again and he said that just wasn't going to happen. Then I said, "Well, at least don't marry somebody else!"

He said, "I *am* going to, and the wedding will be next month."

It's not that I don't like Ramona (she's my dad's girlfriend). She's okay. I was

scared when I first met her, and she told me she was scared when she first met me, too.

Once, at a school taco dinner, someone asked me if Ramona was my mother and I said, "My parents are divorced, so this ISN'T my mother." My dad told me later that he didn't like the way I said it, and I said, "So?"

He gave me a time-out.

I don't exactly know when Dad and Ramona began dating. I just noticed that suddenly Dad was gone a lot and came home happy. When I asked him why, he said that he still felt sad and angry about the divorce, but that he wanted to meet new people.

Ramona's girls are named Raquel, who is eleven years old, and Rosa, who is seven. They have a cat named Purr-fecto. I have a bird named Tweedie.

I just don't think this is going to work!

Rosa is a spoiled brat. Whatever she wants, she gets, if she yells long enough. She'll probably come into my room and take my stuff and be a pest. Raquel thinks she's the boss just because she is older. I liked it better when *I* was the oldest. My dad is going to adopt the girls after he and Ramona get married. Gross!

I wonder if my dad and Ramona will have a baby? That would be the worst idea in the world!

One day Ramona said she wanted to take me to the zoo. She said she would get a baby-sitter for the girls. It would be just the two of us. I hate to admit it, but we had a really good time.

I didn't tell my mom that I liked Ramona because it would have hurt Mom's feelings. My dad said that liking Ramona doesn't mean I don't love my mom.

Dad keeps calling the wedding "our wedding." I am sick of hearing about it. It's going to be in a church, and MILLIONS of people are coming. The girls and I are going to be in the wedding ceremony. They are all excited about wearing fancy dresses. I am NOT excited about wearing a tuxedo and having everybody say, "Oooooh, you're SO cute"!

At the wedding we will each get a medallion that says, "FAMILY." I would rather have sports cards.

After the wedding Dad and Ramona went on their honeymoon for a week and I stayed with Mom. She cried all week. When Dad and Ramona came back I moved into the new house. It's a great house except that the girls live there, too!

I go to a new school, so I'll probably never see any of my friends again. And my new teacher gives too much homework. My grades aren't the greatest now.

Maybe if I were a little bit older I wouldn't feel so bad about my dad getting married again. Dad said that whatever is good for parents is good for the children. I don't think that is true.

I don't want to call Ramona "Mom." She's NOT my mom. She said that I can call her Ramona and that she knows I already have a mother. She's pretty smart for a stepmother.

I don't know what to call Rosa and Raquel, either. Are they my sisters, or do I tell people they are my "stepsisters"?

Ramona said I don't have to love the girls but she would like me to try to get along with them. I will, as long as they stay out of my room!

There is one great thing about moving to our new house. My grandma lives one block away! She is my dad's mother and I like her a LOT.

She listens to me and never tells me how I should feel about anything. I like my other grandmother, too, but I don't get to see her anymore since the divorce.

My Grandmother likes Rosa and Raquel and Ramona, but she says it's okay for me to visit her without them.

She said to tell her when I'm ready for Rosa and Raquel to come with me.

When I came back from Grandma's house today, Ramona was crying. She said she was tired of miniature golf and hot dogs, and wanted more time alone with my dad.

Rosa and Raquel are mad because their mom tries so hard to make friends with me. One day, Ramona was helping me and Raquel said, "Forget about ME, Mom. I'm just your REAL daughter!"

Sometimes I get mixed up about rules at my mom's house and here. Once, Ramona said, "I don't know what your mother told you, but at this house we're CLEAN!" Usually she doesn't say bad things about my mom. Good thing!

Most of the time my dad tells *me* what to do and Ramona tells *Rosa and Raquel* what to do. It works a lot better that way.

Sometimes my dad tries too hard to make Rosa and Raquel like him. Once, he said, "I bet your other dad didn't take you fishing."

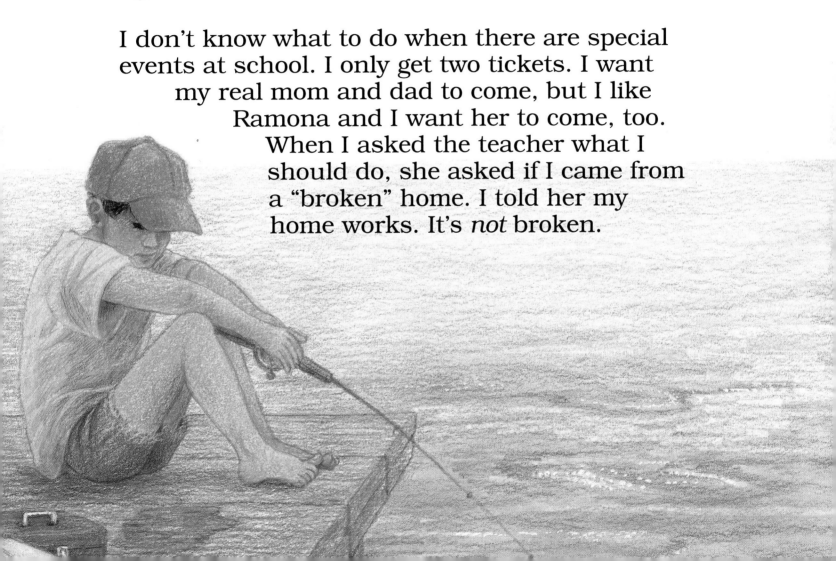

And sometimes I don't let Ramona be nice to me because I don't care if she and Dad get a divorce. Then my mom and dad can get married again.

I don't know what to do when there are special events at school. I only get two tickets. I want my real mom and dad to come, but I like Ramona and I want her to come, too. When I asked the teacher what I should do, she asked if I came from a "broken" home. I told her my home works. It's *not* broken.

We've started having Family Night at home. First we have the meeting. It's great! Everybody gets a turn and we can say what bothers us, and then we talk about what we can do to make our family work better. Then Ramona and Dad say something nice about everybody. After that we do something fun together, like go skating, and then get hamburgers on the way home.

One day at school I was chosen "Student of the Week." When I ran in the house after school, I said, "Mom, guess what happened!" Ramona smiled a really big smile and said, "That sounded very nice, son." Then she cried. Parents are pretty strange sometimes.

Rosa and I play together. Raquel gets mad about that sometimes because she thinks Rosa should only play with her.

Rosa's not bad, for a sister. Both of us go over to Grandma's house now. Raquel could come if she would quit being a brat. Grandma's real smart. She says, "Love can't be forced."

Sometimes Ramona and my dad fight. It's just like what happened before my parents got a divorce. It really scares me. What if Dad and Ramona get divorced? I asked my grandma if the fighting was my fault, and she said that grownup fighting is NEVER the kids' fault. After Dad and Ramona have a fight, they kiss and make up. It's embarrassing.

April 10 was Rosa's birthday. I thought it would be like my birthday, but it wasn't. It was weird.

Ramona made a big cake and we had a party, and that night we had to eat whatever Rosa picked for dinner. We had spaghetti, three kinds of ice cream, and potato chips.

It has been almost one year since our new family began. We are going to have a celebration next week. In some ways I still feel sad about my mom and dad getting a divorce, but I like my new family, too. Sometimes Ramona says I look just like my mom. I like that. She will always be my mom but my new mom is really nice, too.

Ramona writes me notes and puts them in my lunch—things like, "You are the best son in the whole world!" I know my dad is happy, and that makes me feel good, too. The only ones who AREN'T happy are Tweedie and my mom.

I have learned a lot this year. One thing is that a stepparent family is not worse or better than other kinds of families. It is simply a DIFFERENT KIND of family.

Dear Friend,

Here are some suggestions for supporting a child who lives in a stepparent family:

1. Encourage stepparents to maintain special time alone with their biological children occasionally, to decrease resentment of the new stepsiblings.

2. Tell stepparents that it's not unusual for children to need as much as five years to accept the new stepparent family, and that some problems will not be apparent in the beginning.

3. Children feel more secure when stepparents agree on methods of discipline, and children are disciplined by biological parents for the first year.

4. Creating new traditions in the stepparent family helps.

5. Warn stepparents that it's easy to avoid facing their own problems by focusing blame on a stepchild's behavior.

6. Never speak critically of the non-custodial parent.

7. Stepparents should plan to spend time alone with stepchildren to begin to build a bond.